This Book Belongs to:

Mickey's
Young Readers Library

VOLUME
10
Donald's Magic Stone

STORY BY MARY PACKARD

Activities by Thoburn Educational Enterprises, Inc.

A BANTAM BOOK
NEW YORK · TORONTO · LONDON · SYDNEY · AUCKLAND

Donald's Magic Stone   A Bantam Book/September 1990. All rights reserved. © 1990 The Walt Disney Company. Developed by The Walt Disney Company in conjunction with Nancy Hall, Inc. This book may not be reproduced or transmitted in any form or by any means.

ISBN 0–553–05625–5

Published simultaneously in the United States and Canada. Bantam Books are published by Bantam Doubleday Dell Publishing Group, Inc. Its trademark, consisting of the words "Bantam Books" and the portrayal of a rooster, is Registered in U.S. Patent and Trademark Office and in other countries. Marca Registrada. Bantam Books 666 Fifth Avenue, New York, New York 10103.

Printed in the United States of America

0   9   8   7   6   5   4   3   2   1

A Walt Disney BOOK FOR YOUNG READERS

One cold winter day, Donald was chopping
wood in his back yard.

"One more log, and I think I'll have enough
wood," said Donald. He was getting very hungry.
The thought of a nice hot dinner was the only thing
that kept him working.

After Donald finished chopping all the wood, he went inside and started to look around his kitchen for some food. But he had forgotten to shop for groceries. There wasn't a single crumb to eat.

"I sure do wish there were some way to get dinner without having to go all the way to the store to buy it," Donald grumbled.

Just then, Donald saw Goofy. Goofy was
walking past the house. In his arms were bags full of
groceries.

Donald thought to himself, "Gee, Goofy has all those groceries. I wonder if there is some way I could get him to invite me to dinner."

Donald raced out of his house. "Goofy! Yoo-hoo! Goofy!" Donald called as he ran.

Suddenly, an unhappy thought popped into Donald's head. He stopped running.

"What if Goofy doesn't invite me to dinner?" worried Donald. "I sure don't want to invite myself. Why, I can't even bring dessert."

Donald thought and thought. Then he noticed a stone sparkling on the ground.

He stared at the stone. Slowly an idea began to take shape.

"That stone looks pretty special," said Donald. "Maybe with a little imagination, I can use this stone to get Goofy to invite me to dinner."

Donald thought for a minute. "I've got it," he cried.

Donald ran after Goofy once again.
"Oh, Goofy!" he called. "Wait for me. I have
something to show you!"
Goofy stopped and waited. He smiled as Donald
raced up to him.

"Did you ever see one of these?" Donald asked.
"Did I ever see a stone?" Goofy asked. "Sure."
"Oh, this is not *just* a stone, Goofy," Donald said
mysteriously. "*This* is a magic stone."

"What does it do?" Goofy asked.

"It makes soup," said Donald. "Do you want to see how?"

"Yes," said Goofy. "Come on over to my house. Let's see if that magic stone can really make soup."

When they got to Goofy's house, the two friends
headed straight for the kitchen. Goofy put the
groceries away and Donald filled a big soup pot
with water.

Donald put the pot of water on the stove to boil.
He dropped the magic stone into the pot. "And now
for the magic words," he said. "Bippity, boppity,
boop. Make a tasty soup!"

Goofy stared at the stone in the pot, waiting for
something to happen.

After a while, the water began to boil. But nothing much else seemed to be happening to the soup.

"You know, Goofy," said Donald, "I've heard that if you add carrots to a pot of stone soup, it makes it taste really delicious."

Donald tasted the soup again. "It's delicious!" he said, smacking his lips loudly.

Then he offered Goofy a taste. Goofy had to agree, it did taste wonderful.

"But you know what it really needs, Goofy?" Donald asked. "This soup would be really special if we added some cabbage. I think stone soup with cabbage is the best soup of all."

Goofy handed Donald the flour, which Donald added to the soup. He stirred, and stirred, and stirred some more, to make sure that the soup would be nice and smooth.

"Hmmm . . ." said Donald, as he looked at the soup. "It isn't as thick as it should be," he added.

Goofy looked worried.

"But I think I know what the problem is," said Donald. "You see, I've made soup with this stone so many times this week that it must be a bit worn out. Maybe a little flour would help."

"Say no more," said Goofy. He walked over to the place where he kept the onions.

Then he and Donald chopped up the onions and stirred them into the soup.

"That soup sure smells good now! Do you think the stone is finished making dinner?" Goofy asked Donald.

Donald took another taste. "Almost," he said. "But I think there's something missing . . ." Donald thought for a minute. "Potatoes!" he decided.

Goofy thought the cabbage was a very good idea. As a matter of fact, he had just bought one at the grocery store that day. So the two friends chopped up the cabbage. Then they added it to the pot.

"Gawrsh, Donald. I have some carrots. Why don't I chop them up and add them to the pot?" Goofy said.

And so he did just that.

The carrots and the water started to boil. Donald lifted a spoonful to cool. Then he took a taste. "Just as I thought, Goofy. This soup will be delicious."

Then Donald added, "But an onion or two would make it taste even better."

"Right!" Goofy agreed. Goofy peeled the potatoes while Donald chopped. Next they poured in the potatoes, and Donald stirred the soup.

Donald stirred the soup some more. Then Donald took another delicious taste.

"Wow! I think this is the best soup I've made all week," Donald called from the kitchen.

"It is?" Goofy asked, as he set the table. His stomach was beginning to growl. "Is it done yet?"

"Not quite yet, Goofy," said Donald. "It still needs a touch of something—but what?" He thought for a minute. "Salt and pepper! That's it! That will make the soup taste perfect."

And so Donald added a bit of pepper and salt.

Donald took one last taste. Then he cried, "Time to eat! The soup is done!"

Goofy sighed happily. "I'm ready when you are," he called from the table, spoon in hand.

Donald looked at the table. He thought the two soup bowls and two soup spoons looked lonely sitting on the table all by themselves.

"You know, Goofy, stone soup goes really well with some bread and butter," Donald said. "And a plate of fine sausages wouldn't hurt, either."

Goofy agreed. So he went through his kitchen, gathering up everything they needed to make a feast.

Before long, Goofy's table was filled with plates of sausages and cheese, fruit and bread, pickles and olives, and whatever else Donald could think of that would go well with the magic stone soup.

At last Donald set the hot soup on the table. He looked at Goofy's happy face. And suddenly, Donald was ashamed of the trick he had played on his friend.

"Goofy, there is something I have to tell you," Donald said. "This stone really isn't magic."

"Sure it is, Donald," said Goofy. "Look how it made my groceries disappear!"

Goofy and Donald laughed together. A little imagination was really all the magic they needed.

Think About It

Magic Stone Soup Recipe

Point to the things Donald used to make his Magic Stone Soup in the order in which Donald put them in the pot. Look back in the story to help you remember the order.

What Do You Think?

1. Was Donald's stone really magic?
2. Why did Donald pretend the stone was magic?
3. Who bought all the food to make the soup?
4. Why was Donald ashamed of his trick?
5. Was Goofy really fooled by the magic stone?

After your child does the activities in this book, refer to the *Young Readers Guide* for the answers to these activities and for additional games, activities, and ideas.

Fun With Words

Soup Words

Point to the things you would use to make your favorite soup.

Spell It Out

The ten food words on Goofy's shopping list are all mixed up. Can you unscramble the letters and figure out the words? (Use the word box to help you.)

ONIONS	BREAD	POTATOES	CARROTS	OLIVES
FLOUR	CABBAGE	BUTTER	SALT	PEPPER

GROCERY LIST

OOINNS
RLOFU
BDAER

BCABGAE
ESOPATTO
UTERBT

RROTCAS
ALST
VIOLES
PPPREE